I0623749

Taken by Two Sugar Daddies

Taken, Volume 15

Jasmine Black

Published by Spunky Girl Publishing, 2023.

Also by Jasmine Black

Taken by Two Sugar Daddies
Taken by Two Elves

The Pleasure Collection
Pleasured by Her Guards
Shared

Standalone
Shared Boxed Set

Taken by Two Sugar Daddies

Jasmine Black
Taken Series

Twenty-two-year-old Liza Cole struggles to pay her many expenses to continue attending a prestigious law school. That is, until she finds a naughty job with an older man who will make her financial troubles go away...she needs to be available to him for business parties as well as available in the bedroom where Liza is quickly taken by *two* Sugar Daddies.

Other stories in the Taken Series by Jasmine Black:

Taken by Two Doctors, Taken by Three Doctors, Taken by Two Bikers, Taken by Three Bikers, Taken by Two Billionaires, Taken by Three Billionaires, Taken by Two Bosses, Taken by Two Cowboys, Taken by Three Cowboys, Taken by Two Firefighters, Taken by Two Carpenters, Taken by Two Personal Trainers, Taken by Two Santas, Taken by Three Bodyguards, Taken by Two Cops, Taken by Two Prison Guards, Taken by Two Lifeguards, Taken by Two Mountain Men, Taken by Two Elves and more!

Copyright

License Notes

This story is licensed for your personal use only.

Author Note

This is a work of fiction. Characters, places, settings, and events presented in this book are purely of the author's imagination and bear no resemblance to any actual person, living or dead or to any actual events, places, and/or settings.

Chapter One

As I gazed across the luxurious dining room at my new employer, Don DeLuca, something naughty inside of me hummed to life. After a bit of research, I'd discovered he was a very successful man in his thirties who owned an online game developer company. Recently he'd given me the opportunity of quitting my low paying waitress job, which I couldn't stand anyway, and come to work for him.

He'd offered me five grand a month and all I had to do was accompany him to his work functions as his date and be there when he needed me for his naughty needs. At first I'd scoffed at the idea of having myself a sugar daddy, but after watching my roommate, Jaz's life get easier when she'd gotten one, I decided I would take the plunge.

Tonight was my first night out with Don. It was a work function for him yet I had no illusions that the evening would end up with him taking me into his bed. The thought kind of scared me yet it thrilled me at the same time. I'd never been with an older man. At twenty-three years of age, I was still inexperienced in the sexual relations department having had sex with only two other guys my age and neither of them had been able to make me orgasm. I'd become quite good at pretending to climax and I was under no illusions that I'd have to do the same with Don.

One of the things he'd insisted on when he'd hired me, was for me to prepare myself anally using an arrangement of butt plugs he'd supplied and be ready to earn my money on our first date. I guess he was into anal and I'd told him the truth that I'd never done that before. He'd smiled and nodded, telling me he'd be gentle until I was broken in.

So tonight I wore a shiny smooth gold plug, the biggest in the package he'd supplied to me. It had taken a couple of weeks to work my way through the arrangement of smaller sizes to this huge one. Now I felt pretty comfortable wearing this plug and I was starting to get excited as I wondered how it might feel having his thick, long, hot cock sliding up into my behind.

My pussy quivered and my ass clenched around the plug as I studied Don. He looked sexy in a black tuxedo. The crisp white shirt brought out the whites in his brown eyes and the shiny black tie complimented his black hair which was combed neatly and parted at the side.

He was throwing a congratulations party for Lloyd Johnson, one of his employees. Lloyd had made it big creating a very popular video game for Don's company. Don offered profit sharing to any employee who produced a successful game for his company and as I'd walked around and talked to Don's guests I'd overheard some of them whispering that Lloyd was now set for life.

I wish I had that problem. Life would be so much easier if I'd been financially set.

I sighed and watched as Lloyd took his position beside Don. Lloyd looked smart dressed in a gunmetal gray suit and he appeared to be in his mid thirties like Don. I don't know why but I couldn't seem to stop my gaze from straying to him instead of keeping my attention on my sugar daddy, but it was what it was.

Lloyd's golden brown colored hair was shaggy and curled low on his neck and his eyes sparkled blue as he lifted a wine goblet to Don's toast. His confident smile to the crowd made my insides tremble and I suddenly wished *he* were my sugar daddy too.

I shook those crazy thoughts aside. I was just a struggling student entering my first year in law school. I'd already completed the necessary years of undergraduate studies and had been accepted into a prestigious law school which I'd quickly realized I wouldn't be able to afford on a waitress salary, especially since my dad had suffered a massive heart attack this past summer and dropped dead right there on the car assembly line where he worked.

I hadn't realized we were broke until my mother, bless her heart, revealed to me that my dad had been taking out mortgages on their house as well as loans to put me and my two younger twin siblings, Larry and Harry, through college. Mom had said he'd really been proud of me and wanted to help me achieve my dream of becoming a criminal defence lawyer for underprivileged minors.

I'd been reeling from the news of my dad's death when my roommate had suggested I go to a party to help cheer me up. A party where it turned out sugar daddies frequented looking for young women who needed financial help and that's where Don and I had first connected.

And so here I was. Gosh, if my dad could see me now, he'd be rolling around in his grave and he'd be so pissed off. His darling little girl, the one he'd been so proud of, was now a sugar baby.

I blew out a tense breath as I shakily lifted my tulip shaped wine glass to join the toast.

"Congratulations to Lloyd," Don said as he gazed at Lloyd with pride flashing in his eyes.

"He came through on delivering a superior product for the company. I am very impressed with his skills and he's set a higher standard for everyone else to meet."

A few nervous chuckles rolled through the crowd as everyone raised their goblet.

I could tell his words were well aimed at his people. Kind of a barbed incentive for them to do better. Or maybe in his own way, fatherly encouragement.

When the toasting was over, the crowd dispersed and returned to mingling with each other.

Don motioned for me to join him at the thirty-foot-long buffet table.

"Here, help yourself to whatever you like, Liza. How are enjoying your evening?" he asked with a smile as I placed my empty glass on a nearby table.

He handed me a stunning gold-trimmed white porcelain plate.

"Plenty of beautiful architecture to admire, especially your crystal chandeliers. They are magnificent."

"Not as magnificent as you, Liza. And I'm sure you will look even hotter when I peel your sexy red dress off you later tonight," he muttered lowly beneath his breath and then winked at me.

My cheeks warmed at his comment. I had no doubt my cheeks would be just as red as my dress by the time he was finished with me tonight.

Don nodded to the elaborate glass buffet table laden with an assortment of food. Then he pointed to the most colorful pizza platters I'd ever seen. The cheese was a gorgeous cream color that drenched the bright green olives, the searing red bits of peppers and toppings I didn't recognize.

"Why don't you try the pizza. It's absolutely one of my favorites. The dough is made from Italy's finest flour and Italian champagne. Toppings include three types of caviar; black, Iranian albino sturgeon and Beluga. It has two different species of lobster; Maine red lobster and Caribbean lobster. The cheese is to die for, made from the goats milk that graze in the high-altitude pastures of Italy.

He didn't wait for me to answer as he grabbed a fancy silver pizza shovel and hefted a large piece and then a second slice onto the plate I held.

"And here, try some of this." He'd moved a few steps ahead and reached down for tongs. He dipped the utensil into a bucket of what appeared to be Caesar's salad. He lifted a generous amount into my plate right next to the pizza.

"This is delicious too, Liza. The croutons are so crisp it will make your head spin. Made from Cook's own secret recipe. He won't even tell *me* how he makes his croutons taste so marvelous," Don chuckled and then continued.

"The romaine hearts are grown organically in Canada's lush Okanagan Valley and they'll literally melt in your mouth. I kid you not. And have some of this Canadian Angus T-bone steak, from Northern Ontario. It is juicy, *Bellissima*."

He looked up at me, put his fingers to his mouth and smacked his lips together. His eyes glittered with such happiness that he reminded me of a child. He was quite excited as he continued placing food onto my plate.

By the time he was finished, my plate was heaped with such an arrangement of foods, I doubted I would be able to eat even a quarter.

"Is this your newest girl? The one we'll be entertaining tonight after the party?"

My breath backed up in my lungs as a deep voice erupted from right behind me. I swallowed and trembled as a hot hand intimately settled upon my lower back. Shock and arousal shot through me when Lloyd tenderly nuzzled the area of my neck between my left earlobe and left shoulder. His warm lips felt smooth upon my flesh and his bristly five o'clock shadow sparkled against tender nerve endings.

To my surprise, my pussy and ass clenched with arousal at his touches.

He smelled good. A rich spicy scent that teased my nostrils.

I knew that voice. It was Lloyd. What did he mean by *we*? And why was he being so bold in the way he was holding me and touching me?

"Lloyd, this is Liza. She's my new girl. Isn't she absolutely beautiful?"

Lloyd let go of me and came around to my front. His gaze flashed with appreciation as he looked at my breasts that brazenly pushed against the tight red dress I wore.

I swallowed as I got the feeling he was literally devouring me with his eyes.

"Lady in Red. She's the flag and we're the bulls," he commented.

Don let out a roaring laugh.

I forced myself to calm down. Of course. Lloyd was just joking. He must be a humorous guy.

For a minute I'd thought I'd have to entertain *two* men tonight. Not that I would mind...but stuff like that was just passing fantasies for me. I would never know how to behave being in bed with two men. I would be so embarrassed!

"Liza and I will be dining privately," Don said.

Whew! I relaxed even more.

"As you say, boss. I'll mingle with the rest of the riffraff for now," Lloyd replied.

He nodded at me and then strolled down to the other end of the long buffet table where a lineup was forming.

Suddenly I realized that Don and I were the only ones at the buffet table and it appeared the rest of the guests of about twenty people were watching us with curious gazes.

I frowned and felt like I was some animal on display.

Did they know I was Don's sugar baby? Or was he discreet?

But Lloyd knew. So maybe the rest of them did too? I'd introduced myself as a friend while I'd mingled.

Oh man, my cheeks were starting to get really hot now as Don nodded for me to follow him. I'd expected him to grab himself a plate and start placing food onto one for himself, but he didn't.

Huh, interesting.

He led me down a long hallway and I looked around.

Draped from the ornate coffee-milk colored twelve-foot-high ceilings were gorgeous sparkling white crystal chandeliers and adorning the white-painted walls were an abundance of oil paintings. Some framed canvases I recognized as the Group of Seven work and there was even an Emily Carr painting.

"Beautiful art," I complimented, knowing each of these paintings had to be worth a fortune.

"Yes, they are all originals. I do have a fetish for Canadian artists and their scenic paintings."

He stopped in front of a set of luxurious doors.

"These are my peacock doors. I commissioned them to look like the famous Peacock doors of the historic Palmer house in Chicago. Made from brass," he commented.

"Absolutely breathtaking," I admitted. Such an intricate design of swirling smooth brass and it all glittered so beautifully beneath the lights of the chandeliers.

Don pushed a black button on the wall and the gorgeous metal doors swung inward to reveal a luxurious room.

At first glance it appeared to be a game room. There was a small cedar jacuzzi in one corner. A fancy pool table in another corner. A large flat screen tv adorned a wall. Nearby a giant stone fireplace flickered warm looking yellow flames and in front of it was a long black leather sofa with a coffee table set in front.

The floor appeared to be wood-planked oak and the walls were a mellow yellow with pretty beachside watercolor painting that hung on the walls. There appeared to be no windows in this room. The lighting were gold sconces that shone a dim glow from various areas of the room.

As I gazed around, I realized this was not just any game room, but a bedroom with a king-sized canopied bed set in the far corner.

"This will be your room on the nights and days you stay over," he said with a wave of his hand and a giant naughty smile on his face.

My tummy hollowed out in a funny kind of way when I noticed *other* items in the bedroom.

Naughty items.

Oh, boy.

This guy sure was serious about his downtime.

Hanging on the walls sprinkled here and there between the pretty beach paintings were floggers, wrist cuffs, spanking paddles, cock rings, cock sleeves, and other adult toys.

Chapter Two

I grinned. It was like being in a sex shop, but discreetly decorated, if that made sense.

"By the smile on your face, you approve?" Don asked.

"I've just never seen something like this. It's quite tastefully decorated," I admitted.

"I'm glad you approve. Any time you see something you want to try; I'll get fresh ones. The ones on the walls are just for browsing, not using."

"Hmm, but when one is in the mood, one doesn't want to wait for fresh ones, am I right?"

I glanced at him. Brightness flashed in his eyes. I could tell he was getting excited.

"The fresh ones are in the adjoining bathroom and will always be in full supply, my dear. Now sit on the sofa and I'll get us some wine. Would you like white again?" he asked as he sauntered over to a well-stocked bar in the far corner of the room. Funny that I hadn't noticed it when I'd first come in.

"Yes, white. I tend to prefer white."

"I will remember that," he said as he walked behind the bar. There was a small fridge there. He opened it and brought out a bottle of white and a bottle of red.

I strolled over to the leather sofa and placed the large dish of food onto the table. The sensual aroma was making my mouth water and I couldn't wait to eat something. The sofa was quite cozy and firm as I sat on it.

Yeah, I could see myself sitting here and enjoying watching tv or doing naughty things to myself when Don was out of the room. Especially now that he'd admitted there were toys in the bathroom.

Truth be told, I loved masturbating because I knew exactly where all my pleasure points were located. I hadn't the money to buy toys so up until now I'd pleasured myself with my fingers. It would be fun to play with toys.

A moment later, Don joined me on the couch. He handed me a goblet of wine and I eagerly sipped the cool drink. Flavors exploded against my taste buds making me moan my appreciation.

"This is really good," I complimented.

He nodded and smiled as he sipped his red wine. I noticed his eyes appeared glass-like and predatory. I trembled in response, instinctively knowing he was thinking of sex.

"Now, before we start to eat, I'd like for you to let me see your breasts."

His instruction was purred so smoothly it took me a moment to decipher what he'd just said.

I blew out a tense breath and to my surprise my pussy tightened in anticipation.

"Sure," I said in a breathy voice. I mean I didn't have much choice, especially since I'd signed up for this and he *was* paying me for the privilege. May as well take the plunge now.

"Could you unzip me?" I asked as I placed my drink upon the table and leisurely turned my back toward him, acting as if I did this sort of thing all the time.

Jaz had told me to always appear confident, but not bold. Sugar daddies liked a woman who wasn't prudish and pushy in the bedroom, she'd said.

I held my breath as he gently pulled the zipper down. Then he tapped my lower back letting me know he was finished.

"You smell very nice, tonight, Liza," he whispered.

"Thank you, Don. But I'm sure it's mostly all this delightful food you picked."

My mouth was suddenly dry as I turned to face him.

He watched eagerly as I reached for my dress straps. Slowly I lowered them over my shoulders and then down my arms. The dress had a built-in bra, and my breasts exploded from the tightness as I lowered the garment.

He inhaled sharply as he stared with appreciation.

Thank you, Jaz! I silently said.

My roommate had loaned me this dress, hence why it was a bit snug. But it appeared Don and Llyod both liked it. It was my mission to make Don like me as that's what Jaz had suggested I be doing if I wanted to keep him as my sugar daddy. It appeared he liked what he saw.

"Beautiful," he whispered. "Very beautiful breasts. So curvy and smooth looking."

His look was definitely appreciative, which made me feel nice.

I wasn't sure if I should say thank you at the compliment, so I remained silent.

"Now, let's eat, shall we. But I want you to wait a moment while I just help myself to a bit of this pizza."

Oh, now I understood why there was so much food in the plate. He'd brought enough for himself too. Silly me, I should have realized that's why.

I waited patiently as he picked up the slice of pizza and took a bite out of it. Strings of cheese flew from the pizza to his mouth and his eyes widened and he made some guttural sounds of approval.

"Mmm, warm but not hot. Perfect for this. Hold still, Liza."

Hold still?

Without warning he reached out and began smearing the pizza all over my left breast and nipple.

My first instinct was to back away, but I held still, remembering Jaz telling me that sugar daddies were unpredictable at best and that I should just enjoy whatever he wanted to do to me because five thousand a month would buy him happiness which I was quite eager to give in order to achieve my goals.

The pizza was nice and warm, but pleasantly so as Don squished the cheese, tomato sauce and other items into one heck of a mashed mess. The sensual way he was massaging me with the pizza erupted naughty sensations into my breast and when he crushed the pizza against my nipple, I felt an arrow of excitement zing between my legs, deep inside my vagina.

Oh, yes, this feels so good!

Instinctively I moaned and thrust my chest against the pizza, craving a harder touch.

"You like that don't you, Liza. I knew you would. Now, I'm sure you'll like this even more," he said.

He placed the pizza back onto the plate and licked his lips.

My body grew hot as he reached out and cupped my left breast. His hand was hot and firm on my flesh, which sent tingles of anticipation through me.

Then he lowered his head.

I moaned as my sugar daddy's hot mouth encircled my pizza-encrusted nipple. He began an intoxicating nibble with his firm lips and then bit gently with his sharp teeth sending erotic sensations through my sensitive bud.

Pleasure and bits of pain zipped through my nipple. My previous boyfriends hadn't done oral on my breasts so I had nothing to compare, but I liked what Don was doing. I liked it a lot.

I gazed down at him and watched his red lips move in rhythmic motion. Sucking sounds split through the air and my breathing grew rough and harsh as breathtaking sensations whipped through me.

I'd never been so sensually aware of things before. Of the pulsing need deep inside my pussy. Of the erotic way my anal muscles clenched the butt plug. Or at how easily I'd submitted to his desire of taking my nipple into his hot mouth.

He sucked harder. More pleasure rippled through me. Soon the pleasure was almost too much to bear. I whimpered my distress.

He slowly let go of my tender flesh and moved his head away. I thought he was going to stop, but then he reached out and grabbed the other slice of pizza and smeared it over and around my other breast, paying special attention to my nipple until it pulsated and I was gasping at the quivering vibrations.

"I love having breasts with my supper," he said in a guttural tone.

His brown eyes sparkled with a savage lust that I found hypnotizing. I didn't realize he'd cupped my other breast until his head once again lowered and I watched my pizza drenched nipple disappear between his plump lips.

I shuddered as he pulled on my nipple with his mouth. Cried out as his teeth nipped. Moaned as his tongue licked and lapped at my sensitive flesh. His growls of appreciation sounded like music in my ears and thrummed like hot lightning through my bloodstream.

When he pulled his head away, both my nipples throbbed and my breasts felt ultra huge.

"You taste of perfection, Liza. I'm so happy you agreed to be with me," he said with a smile.

"What's not to like?" I said breathlessly.

I figured he was finished feasting on my breasts and made a move to lift my dress straps but he shook his head.

"Leave your breasts exposed, darling. I like to watch them while I feed you."

Oh, he was going to feed me? Ookay. With my upper half naked. This was going to be different and a bit embarrassing.

"But first, we'll need some cutlery. I have it at the bar. Back in a second."

I nodded and watched as he stood and then sauntered over to the bar.

My focus drew down to my breasts.

Don had licked them clean of any pizza evidence. My nipples appeared plump and red and my breasts looked much bigger, just like they felt.

As Don walked back toward me, I couldn't help but notice the huge bulge displayed between his thighs and I trembled with both excitement and a tinge of fear. What if I didn't perform good enough in bed for him? Would my goals be dashed even before they'd started?

"Why the sad look, my dear? Did you not enjoy what I did?" he asked in a concerned voice as he set the cutlery down beside the plate of food and sat down beside me.

"Oh, yes, I did. I was just..." I couldn't tell him the truth. That I was feeling insecure with a low confidence in my abilities.

I quickly forced a smile.

"I was just thinking that I would like to return the favor sometime."

Dear heavens, had I just said that? Why did I say that? I'd never had a man's nipple in my mouth. Never entertained the thought. Until now.

His face brightened.

"How about we save that for another time? I'm famished."

Shit. I'd been too bold. I needed to tone it down. He was paying, so he was in charge.

I nodded.

I waited for him to start feeding me. I'd finally begun to realize I needed to take his cue on pretty much everything, or I would blow that five grand a month. My nervousness intensified at my self-inflicted pressure to be perfect.

"We will try the steak first. It goes wonderfully with white wine," he said as he cut up the meat and pierced a piece with his fork.

He aimed that steak at my face and I opened my mouth quickly and allowed him to push the food past my slightly parted lips. Intense flavor burst against my tastebuds and I couldn't help but moan at the arrangement of spices that made love to my mouth

"There you go, baby. Now chew it nice and good."

I blinked and began to chew. Did he just call me baby? Was that like an endearing compliment or was he now role playing? I'd heard some guys got off on being a mom to a baby.

He speared some of the Caesar salad and came at my mouth again. Quickly I swallowed the meat and opened wide, accepting the food. I couldn't help but moan again as garlic and onions and all kinds of delicious tastes melted onto my tongue.

"You like that? Good isn't it? I like the way your lips part when I feed you. So sensual. So inviting," he whispered.

Oh, oh. He had that intense sexual stare again.

Sex was on his mind. I gazed longingly at the food on the tray as he lifted my goblet of wine and brought it to my lips. I felt self-conscious as I sipped the sweet wine while he watched.

"More, baby," he whispered after I stopped sipping.

I drank some more and stopped. And then he nodded that I keep drinking.

So I did and soon I felt the buzz of the booze take the nervous edge off me. He poured me another glass and made me sip more.

Was he trying to get me drunk?

Suddenly he moved the glass away.

He placed the wine glass onto the nearby table, and then I gasped as he reached out with both his hands and cupped my breasts. His hands were hot as he held my mounds and then his thumbs were sensuously stroking over my hardening nipples creating an awesome friction that sent arrows of pleasure darting into my pussy.

My breaths grew faster and my senses spun as he lowered his head, his lips coming toward my mouth.

Oh geez. My sugar daddy was going to kiss me!

My mind whirled as his lips covered mine, determinedly and forcefully.

Sensations sizzled through me as Don kissed me harder, his mouth slanting over mine in a heady possession. His tongue forced my lips apart and sank into my mouth like a missile. Our tongues clashed and his dominated mine; touching and thrusting like he owned me.

The heat of my excitement weakened me and I found my hands curling over his shoulders, pulling his hot body against me, suddenly needing to touch him. He possessed muscles beneath his tuxedo. I could feel them press against my fingers and my soft curves.

He was strong. Very strong as he easily pushed me back against the sofa.

He lifted his leg over mine and then he was straddling me. I shuddered as his heavy arousal pressed naughtily against my lower belly.

I whimpered as his hands massaged my breasts and he kissed me so passionately and so swiftly that my head was spinning. The intimate way his lips made love to mine made my pussy quiver. I felt so hot that I swear I was about to gyrate my aroused pussy against his engorged package, when a man's voice stopped me cold.

"Looks like you started the party without me."

Chapter Three

The voice came from directly above and behind me and I recognized it instantly. Embarrassment lashed my senses. I could smell his rich spicy scent as it teased my nostrils.

It was Lloyd.

Don tore his mouth from mine and cursed softly, mumbling about not expecting Lloyd so soon.

So soon? What did he mean by that?

My heart began to pound as I remembered their earlier conversation by the buffet table.

Quickly Don let go of my breasts. His brown eyes flashed with excitement as he climbed off me. I made a grab to cover myself with the dangling top part of my dress, but Don's hands snapped like handcuffs around my wrists stopping me cold.

"Don't hide yourself. I want him to see my new sugar baby," Don murmured as he let go of my wrists.

I had a closeup view of his pants and I simply could not believe how tented it had become from his erection. How in the world could a man get so big so fast?

He strolled away and I noted Lloyd had taken Don's place right in front of me.

Embarrassment fused into my cheeks as Lloyd stared down at me. His intense blue gaze was hot and fixated upon my bared breasts.

Before I knew it, he was down upon his knees right in front of me.

"Lloyd is a pussy man," Don said. He'd moved back to the bar and appeared to be pouring a drink.

I was...stunned. How could Don act so casually with another man in the room with us?

"I hope you don't mind, I invited Lloyd to join us this evening. He's interested in getting a sugar baby for himself, now that he'll be rolling in money," Don said casually.

Oh my goodness! This was getting quite overwhelming. Exactly what did Don expect me to do with Lloyd?

"Hey sweetheart, don't look so spooked. We know how to make you feel really good," Lloyd said in a low husky voice. He stared at me with predatory eyes. I wasn't sure if I should be afraid of that look or be grateful that he was so interested in me.

"Why don't we get the rest of your dress off, so the bulls can have some fun with the lady in red," Don said with a chuckle as he handed Lloyd a glass that contained a liquid with a brownish hue.

I could smell it was whiskey. My dad used to drink a glass of whiskey after he came home from the night shift at the plant where he worked. He said it helped him get to sleep faster.

But these two men didn't appear to want to sleep tonight.

I hadn't been expecting this. Really I hadn't. To be displayed like this before two virtual strange men. And yet I did remember a conversation when Don had interviewed me for the job asking if I was comfortable with threesomes. I had said yes. Heck, I would have said yes to anything for five grand a month! I just hadn't expected to be confronted with a threesome on my first night!

"On the other hand, she should have some more food before we proceed. She'll need the energy," Don said as he sat down beside me on the sofa. I watched as he lifted the fork and stabbed a giant piece of that delicious steak he'd fed me earlier. But to my surprise, he lifted it to Lloyd's lips. Lloyd didn't even hesitate as he opened his mouth and accepted the food.

I stared in stunned disbelief as he chewed and the two men smiled at each other. Twinkles of cheerfulness in their eyes and caring gazes.

Were they gay? Not that there was anything wrong with that. I just hadn't expected this connection between them either.

"That's good isn't it, my baby?" Don murmured sweetly to Llyod, who eagerly nodded and sipped on his whiskey as he chewed. My gaze fixated to Lloyd's wet mouth. His dark five o'clock shadow made him look so dangerous and sexy. I loved the way his lips moved so sensually. It kind of made me want those luscious looking lips sucking on my pussy.

Wow, that idea had come out of nowhere. But yeah, the thought of Lloyd's face buried between my legs turned me on!

Lloyd was still kneeling on the floor between my legs and I held my breath as I watched him reach out his free hand. I whimpered as he slid it between my parted knees. His hand disappeared beneath my red dress and smoothed along my inner left thigh creating quite an intoxicating sensation as he leisurely stroked his fingers along my trembling flesh toward my pussy and continued to sip on his whiskey acting as if it was every day he did such a wicked thing.

I exhaled slowly at the intimate gesture, trying to keep calm as wonderful sensations zipped along my thigh up toward my now throbbing and eager pussy. Heat sparked inside my vagina and cream gushed down my channel.

I didn't wear panties as per his previous instruction when he'd given me those butt plugs. He said no bras and no panties. Ever. Now I knew why. My pussy was sopping wet with arousal as I imagined having both men's cocks pistoning into me.

"Open wide, baby," Don purred. I thought he meant my legs which I'd already automatically opened, but another piece of steak was poised at my mouth. I could barely see it as my eyelids had grown so heavy with lust.

I opened as per his instruction and moaned as the incredible flavors once again exploded against my taste buds.

"I like that sound, baby. Lloyd, make her do more of those sexy sounds. They turn me on," Don breathed.

I moaned again as Lloyd's fingers tenderly brushed against my ultra-sensitive clitoris.

"And since I'm a breast man, and I love my breasts blushing, I'll be back in a minute," Don said.

I could hardly hear Don's words as heated blood pounded in my ears.

Lloyd's fingers had begun a sensual rub over my throbbing clitoris and I could barely gather the question together in my head as to what Don meant about breasts blushing because right now all I could feel was the arousal pounding my pussy and the array of flavors bursting inside my mouth as I chewed the steak.

My vagina clenched as Lloyd slipped in a finger. He withdrew quickly and I realized he'd gathered some wetness from me to use as lube because his finger moved more easily now as he continued to massage my clit.

"Told you that you'd start to feel really good," Lloyd whispered a moment later as he suddenly stopped.

I whimpered my distress as he moved his fingers away, leaving my pussy feeling so heavy and achy.

I blinked down at him and tensed as he placed his empty whiskey glass on the nearby table and then returned his focus on me. He lifted my dress exposing my pussy to him.

"A very nice juicy pussy we have here," Lloyd murmured as he gazed between my legs.

The heat at the juncture of my thighs was quickly becoming a fire. I blew out a quick breath, feeling flushed and way too warm.

"Ahh, I see you're making yourself acquainted with my baby, dear boy, Lloyd," Don said as he strolled out of the bathroom. He was holding his left hand behind his back and he held something he was going to be using on me. He had said earlier there were toys in the bathroom.

Oh boy, this was getting intense so quickly.

"She's ripe and quite red. I see you've outfitted her with a plug too. Very impressive," Lloyd said without looking up.

"Thank you," Don replied.

"She looks scrumptious," Lloyd whispered.

I simply couldn't believe what I was hearing. They were talking about me like I was a piece of fruit or something.

"While you explore our sugar baby, I'll get Liza into a more comfortable position," Don said as he moved to stand beside Lloyd.

"Liza, baby. Please extend one of your hands."

I blinked as he produced handcuffs. Not cop style cuffs. These were red and furry. He shoved a key into a metal slot, and the cuffs immediately opened.

I remembered I *did* agree to all kinds of naughty things when he'd interviewed me.

My thoughts disintegrated as Lloyd's head began to lower between my spread legs.

Anticipation screamed through me and I held out a hand. The cuff quickly snapped shut over my wrist.

"The other one, please," Don said.

I nodded jerkily as Lloyd's face got closer to my pussy. Heavens, I could feel his hot breath stroking my intimate areas!

Without thinking I stretched out my other arm.

Another snap of the cuffs. I was barely aware of my arms being raised over my head as Lloyd's tongue lapped at my outer labia folds creating an incredible tension inside my lower belly.

"We'll just restrain you while we enjoy ourselves," Don said rather coolly.

That's when I heard a tinkle of chains from up above. My head snapped upward and I spied a chain dangling from the ceiling and it was attached to my handcuffs! I was effectively restrained! The question of where had that chain come from zipped through my mind.

I pulled on the cuffs but I only had a couple of inches of leeway. I could also see that this new position had thrust my breasts up and out, making them look even bigger.

Oh boy. I was now at their mercy.

"I can read the question in your eyes. I have buttons that I can push on this remote to bring chains down in certain areas of this room," he explained and nodded to a remote control on the coffee table that I thought had been for the television set.

"That way all is ready when I wish to use it," he said proudly.

Okay. The guy was rich. I guess he could pay for all kinds of things. Must be nice.

My mouth grew dry with nervousness as Don lifted a crop from the table. I had been so enamoured by Lloyd's face between my thighs and then focused on the cuffs; I hadn't noticed he'd also brought along a crop. The crop was made from leather as I could smell the scent wafting through the air and mingling with the aroma of my arousal. One end of the crop had a wide head and it had a long handle and it was black. It looked new too.

"I'm going to make those lovely breasts blush, Liza," he said with a hungry grin.

I felt my mouth drop open in surprise.

"Will it hurt?" I asked meekly, suddenly realizing my mistake. I'd just revealed to him my inexperience in the bdsm department.

"Don't worry. I'm just going to tap your pretty little nipples and your smooth breasts, until all is as red as your hot dress, but first..."

My breasts as red as my dress? That didn't sound very exciting.

He'd stopped talking and I watched as he reached downward to his zipper. I heard the rasp of it being lowered.

I gasped in shock as his giant cock exploded from the garment.

Don sighed in apparent relief and my heart sped up at the immense size of him.

His penis quickly angled upward toward his belly.

Oh, my. Yes, he certainly was big. Maybe ten inches long. Maybe longer. He possessed a wide girth of maybe two inches that was riddled with pulsing blue veins and topped with a giant mushroom shaped cockhead.

Despite my shock at his immense size, my pussy and ass tightened wonderfully.

From between my thighs, Lloyd chuckled.

"That clenching is exactly the reaction I am looking for. Her pussy and her ass do love the look of your cock," he said as he kept gazing at my pussy.

Don smiled and winked down at me.

"I knew she would. But my cock will only get bigger from here on out."

Sweet mercy! I couldn't believe he could get *any* larger than what he'd already gotten. I sure hoped he was just kidding.

I held my breath and tensed as Don suddenly flicked the crop downward. The head of the crop slapped just outside the left side of my left nipple, causing a sharp sting.

I gasped at the intriguing sensations the smack caused.

"The trick is to go nice and slow so we can release your endorphins. To alternate between light and slow and fast and hard taps. To tease the outer edges of the nipple and bring it to life. From my experience some women don't like having their nipples cropped. So with you, we will have to test and discover your limits and your endurance."

Oh great, I was a guinea pig.

I tensed once more as he flicked the crop again, and then again, tapping and snapping all around the outer edges of my nipple until wicked heat was blossoming through my breast and I was yelping and squirming from the naughty sensations each blow caused.

My flesh stung and to my surprise I enjoyed the heady buzz the stings fashioned. Or maybe the buzz had been created by the wine? Nonetheless, I liked where this was going.

I became focused on my nipple as he suddenly flicked the crop right upon it. I hissed at the zip of pain, but then the pain quickly vanished and turned into a pulsing throb. Again and again, the gentle slap of the crop rained upon my flesh. My nipple swiftly turned hard and beaded up like a pretty little red rosebud.

It pulsated and ached beneath every light blow and before I knew it I was moaning in response to the sizzling sensations zipping through my breast and arrowing down my belly deep into my vagina making me cream even harder.

I was so fixated on how beautiful my nipple looked like as if it were a clenched flower against my flushing red flesh, that I didn't notice Lloyd had moved his face even closer.

I bucked my hips as he suddenly fused his mouth over my entire wet pussy. His tongue quickly darted like a mini-cock into my vagina and I shuddered beneath the onslaught of arousal whipping through me.

Just as quickly as he thrust his tongue into me, he withdrew and lapped and slurped around my labia lips and then my clitoris creating such pleasure that I found myself keening.

Wet slurpy sounds along with my keening pounded the air as he plunged his long tongue into my vagina and began an erotic pistoning. I tipped my pelvis upwards to get a harder contact with his mouth but his hands came upon my thighs, his fingers digging into my flesh as he held me down. Pleasure was gathering like a firestorm deep inside of me and I wanted to come so bad, but then he pulled out. Just like that.

The pressure of his hot mouth disappeared and his tongue was gone, leaving me moaning and gyrating my hips against his strong hands.

Wow. I really wanted him. Needed him. Craved for him to penetrate me.

Chapter Four

"**S**he is delicious," Lloyd said as he lifted his face away and looked up at Don who'd stopped smacking me with the crop.

Lloyd was licking his glossy lips like he'd just enjoyed a treat.

Don nodded and smiled at him.

"I bet she is delightful," Don replied. "I can smell her from here. She's a breath of fresh air, isn't she. My other sugar babies would have been crying at this point. But Liza appears to enjoy having her breast and nipple cropped. It is a delightful change indeed to have a woman who can handle some pain with her pleasure."

"Please, carry on. I'd like to see how much more she can take while I feast upon her," Lloyd said softly as he nodded at me.

His blue eyes were really dark now. Like the aqua blue coloring in swimming pools. His eyelids were drooping with lust and then his face disappeared between my thighs. I convulsed as his mouth seared over my vaginal opening like a vice.

He began sucking the cream from me and quickly drew me toward an orgasm, but then he backed off as if knowing exactly how much pressure to give me to keep me on this side of sanity and to prevent me from climaxing.

The man was a devil with his tongue and his lips!

Slurping, licking and laving. He was making me nuts as I writhed and bucked loving the way his mouth made love to my pussy. Loving the incredible pleasure that was threatening to overwhelm me at any second.

I CRIED OUT AND PULLED against the restraints as Don began to pummel my other breast with the crop. My need for penetration mounted as both men continued their sensual assault upon my senses and my body. Pleasure, pain, heat and need were zipping everywhere the two men touched.

I was a pussy. I was a breast. I wasn't me anymore.

It was amazing. Yet at the same time, it was torture.

Don kept up a steady pace thrashing me with the crop. Before long, both my breasts felt oh so very hot and my nipples were hard like little glass pebbles. My pussy easily gave my pleasure cream to Lloyd who just kept on sucking.

"Oh yes, you're really blushing beautifully now, Liza," Don drawled.

I must have entered some kind of otherworldly high or drugged state of mind from this pleasurable torture, because suddenly Don's aroused voice cut into my mind.

Lloyd had stopped making love to my pussy with his mouth and Don had discontinued his cropping, but it still felt like they were doing it. My flesh tingled and burned with fever. My ass and pussy were clenching empty air and my nipples felt so hard I swear they might shatter if one of the men so much as touched them.

"Hey, baby girl, why don't you open your eyes and see what kind of treat we have for you," Don said.

I tried to do as he instructed but my eyelids were so heavy. I moaned as I smelled that pizza from earlier. These guys were truly freaking out my senses and keeping me off balance. Sex one minute and food the next.

"Open your mouth, sweetie. Time for some nourishment and wine," Lloyd coaxed from somewhere nearby.

Goodness, I must have gone insane. I hadn't climaxed and yet I felt as if I was in some euphoric state.

Numbly I opened my mouth, a piece of my common sense listening to what Don had said. Nourishment. Yes, I would need substance to see me through this erotic night.

Flavours spun into my mouth as I chewed on the pizza. I swear I had never tasted something so delicious. It was followed by a healthy dose of Caesar's salad and then sips of wine that literally made love to my taste buds.

I felt heady. I wasn't me anymore. Something inside of me had changed. It was like the armour I'd wrapped myself in since my dad had died was dissolving. I liked being fed. Liked being taken care of in this way. I hadn't felt safe since he'd died.

Lloyd and Don fed me until I was satisfied and then I sipped on some more wine. Finally I was able to open my eyes. I gazed down and looked at my breasts.

Have mercy! They were so pink! My nipples so engorged.

"Looks lovely, don't they, Liza," Don murmured as he placed my empty wine glass down on the table.

"How are your arms? Are they sore?" he asked.

I shook my head. I'd forgotten they were upstretched. Why wasn't I in pain?

"Good. It will make it easier for us to do this," Don said. He nodded to Lloyd, who quickly sat down on one side of me. Don sat on my other side.

Suddenly I felt self-conscious as both men turned toward me and stared at my breasts. Instinctively I knew what they were going to do.

My breaths came faster as both men reached out and cupped my tender breasts with their large palms. Then their heads lowered and I cried out and impulsively pulled on the restraints as each man's hot lips enveloped a nipple.

Sensations and pleasure threw me right back into erotic euphoria as the men suckled at my breasts. Their tongues were lapping and licking at the exquisitely tender tips and their hands were caringly massaging my flesh until I was moaning and instinctively gyrating my hips.

My pussy and my anus tightened. Wetness soaked me between my thighs. Their free hands began to roam naughtily over my stomach, my abdomen, and along my inner thighs. Sharp anticipation careened throughout me. I widened my legs praying someone would touch my clitoris or penetrate me with their finger.

But they didn't. Their hands just kept roving along my body, their lips twisting and suckling on my nipples.

I could feel the length of Don's hot, solid penis rubbing against my outer thigh.

Oh, I wanted his cock to come into me so bad.

I found it hard to breathe, as I was gasping so fast while the two men stroked my body. The suckling sounds were splitting through the air like music and their heavily aroused breaths were coming rough and loud.

Yeah, I liked this. Having two men's mouths sucking on my tender, engorged nipples. Their hard palms and exploring fingers sliding over my smooth, tender flesh shooting awareness and arousal throughout my entire body.

I wished this would go on forever.

But all too soon their mouths and hands were leaving me and I was crying out for them to come back.

My nipples throbbed from the stimulation of their mouths and my mind was splintering, my thoughts disappearing into some unknown vortex as my need for penetration continued to grow.

"Now I'm just going to lower your arms so you can be free, and I want you to move to the end of the sofa," Don instructed.

I could barely hear him; the blood was rushing so loudly in my ears. And I could really smell my arousal as it wafted up from between my wet thighs. Could feel the heat and the hot cream oozing from me as my arms were lowered. I wanted to reach down between my legs and bring myself to climax, but the chain would only lower my arms to a certain point. Not far enough to touch myself.

Frustration destroyed me and I moaned my distress.

Lloyd grinned at me, satisfaction sparkling in his blue gaze as he placed a bunch of pillows at the end of the sofa, right against the armchair. And as I numbly began to move toward those pillows, I was surprised when Don let me off the chain, finally allowing me to bring my arms all the way down. He quickly undid my wrists from the restraints and before I could so much as think to touch my clit and get myself off, Don helped move me along the couch, his hands curling under my armpits as he efficiently pulled me to the far end.

Then he swung my legs up and I fell onto my belly. My legs were stretched out behind me on the sofa and my breasts and belly were cradled and my ass was high against the abundance of soft pillows. My head was upraised and my chin settled snugly upon the armchair.

Have mercy, but Don was a strong man. He'd easily picked up my legs and swung me into the position and now he quickly grabbed my arms and spread them apart. Then came the tinkle of chains from somewhere below the sofa. He snapped a single soft black leather cuff over my right wrist and bent my arm at the elbow, bringing my hand down. I heard a click and suspected he'd secured me once again. I tried to move my arm, but it only moved an inch.

I wasn't afraid at all. If they'd wanted to do something bad to me, they could have done it earlier.

Another tinkle of chain followed. He swiftly cuffed my left wrist and secured me the same way as my other arm.

Restrained again!

"Okay, let's have some more fun with our sugar baby, shall we, Lloyd?" Don snickered.

Our sugar baby? Interesting choice of words. But I shook away the idea of having two sugar daddies. I didn't think I would have the energy to be at the sexual beck and call of two men on a daily basis. I'd never be able to go to school, let alone study! I'd be exhausted! But what I was thinking was just a fantasy. Don most likely wanted me all to himself most of the time...unless the two men were bisexual?

And if they are bi, why not indulge yourself in the pleasures they have to offer? My inner voice teased. *They do make you feel very aroused.* But I'd wait to see how tonight went before I suggested having threesomes on a nightly basis. Oh shoot, here I was being bold again. Don was the man paying me. I would have to do what he wanted. Not what I wanted.

The rustle of clothing had me tense as I wondered what was going on now? I turned my head and could barely see Lloyd as he was partially standing behind Don.

My breath jammed as I caught a glimpse of what Llyod was doing. He was lowering his pants!

Before I could see his cock emerge, a sharp smack zipped across my left buttock cheek.

I yelped in surprise.

Don chuckled as he caressed his sizzling hot palm across the area of my flesh that he'd just struck. His hand was gentle and his touch eased the sting the crop had just caused.

"You're going to love this, Liza. I'll have your ass as red as your dress in no time flat and then I'll take your ass," Don said in a deep husky voice. His hand moved away.

I'll take your ass. His words made me shudder with both fear and anticipation as I imagined his long thick shaft penetrating my virgin behind.

Another smack of the crop made all thoughts fly away. A naughty sting followed where he'd just struck. The pain subsided and heat zipped along the area he'd hit.

Okay, I could do this. I'd endured and liked having my nipples and breasts cropped and those areas still burned beautifully. I smiled. Yes, I was going to enjoy another good thrashing.

I tensed as Don began cropping my quivering bared ass.

But then hot pulsing lust shot through me as Lloyd came around and stood directly in front of me. He was naked from the waist down. He held his thick, long erection in one hand and he was stroking the length of his cock with the fingers of his other hand.

I swallowed as nervousness shot through me. His shaft was just as big as Don's!

And Lloyd was aiming his cock right at my mouth!

"Suck it," he commanded in a harsh tone.

I was stunned at his size as I stared up along his shaft. Would some of him even fit into my mouth? He had to be at least ten inches long like Don and I suspected his girth could be more than two inches! The length of his shaft was flushed a pretty shade of reddish-purple and his cockhead did look like a giant purple grape with a big slit in it.

I did love grapes and I could pretend I was sucking on one. I giggled to myself at that thought. His scrotum looked pretty swollen too. And heavy, ready to release his seed.

I was glad I was on the birth control pill because these guys weren't going to be using condoms. It was one of the prerequisites of our deal and Don had assured me he didn't have any diseases and neither would any of the men he'd want me to be with. He had a reputation to uphold, he'd said.

Gosh, had that conversation been less than a month ago? I'd spoken with my roomie Jaz about what Don had wanted from me and about his assurances concerning his sexual health. She'd asked around for me, and I'd met up with a couple of his previous sugar babies. The women had been pretty and they'd looked a bit like me.

They'd had only good things to say about Don. That he'd pleased them in the bedroom and they'd never contracted any diseases from him or his buddies.

"Open up, sugar baby. Let's see how good you are," Lloyd said with a growl as he pressed his erection against my closed lips.

His voice ripped me back to the present and his words seemed to challenge me. Defiance and lust shone through me. I would show Lloyd that the money Don was paying me was worth it.

I yelped as Don cropped my ass again. This time a bit harder. The strike left a beautiful burn on my left buttock cheek and made my pussy quiver with eagerness.

"Come on, baby. Let's open that gorgeous mouth," Lloyd urged.

Hmm, he sounded desperate. I gazed up at him. His face was twisted with arousal. His blue eyes were heavy-lidded and his cheeks quite flushed. The idea that he was so turned on, turned me on even more.

Fevered heat whipped through me. I parted my lips and he slowly slid his giant grape-shaped cockhead into my mouth.

Chapter Five

I felt my eyes widen in surprise as his size stretched my muscles quite a bit and soon touched the back of my throat against my tonsils. He withdrew about an inch and then he wrapped his hand around the wide base of his shaft before sliding his hot, solid flesh out of my mouth. He poised his cockhead upon my lips.

It felt velvety smooth, just like a grape and throbbed against my lips. I gazed up at him again and was stunned to see his mouth hanging open and his eyes tightly scrunched as if he were in pain.

"It appears as if you like her sweet little mouth," Don chuckled to Lloyd. I winced as the crop came down on one ass cheek again, leaving a pleasure burn in it's wake.

"Hot, succulent and oh so very tight," Lloyd answered him in a tense voice.

"Her pretty mouth is the first thing I noticed when I saw her," Don answered.

I wished my hands were free. I had a craving to run my fingertips along Lloyd's smooth-looking, engorged penis. Instead I clenched my fists with inner frustration.

The crop fell across my butt cheek again bringing with it another naughty sting and I impulsively tightened my mouth around Lloyd's shaft. My ass also got into the action, clenching around that big butt plug I wore.

Lloyd cursed softly in response.

"You did that on purpose," he complained to Don.

Don laughed cheerfully and struck my buttock again. Every blow seemed harder and hotter. I had to admit, I did like the pleasure pain he created and enjoyed how my lips constricted around Lloyd's pulsing erection with each strike.

"Okay, sweet baby, start sucking," Lloyd murmured.

He pressed his shaft a bit deeper into my mouth and I tightened my cheeks and lips and began a slow, seductive suck. His shaft really stretched and burned my lips and pretty soon he was doing an erotic pistoning.

I began to bob my head as well, causing a nice rubbing all while taking more of him into my mouth, allowing his grape-shaped cockhead to touch the back of my throat. I enjoyed the smooth tip, and every time he pulled back, I licked at the precum on his slit, enjoying the salty flavor.

Salty grapes. I'd never look at another big grape in the same way again.

To my surprise, Lloyd sifted the fingers of his free hand into my hair at the top of my head and twisted the strands until they burned my scalp. He held tight and bucked his hips, making me suck his pulsing flesh harder and deeper.

He thrust between my lips over and over, faster and faster until my lips tingled and felt oh so beautifully bruised.

Mercy, did he ever fill my mouth with his hot flesh. I could smell his musky scent. Could feel the intense throbbing against my tongue as he continued to thrust between my lips, but he was starting to slow down. I sensed he didn't want to come. At least not yet.

So, I began to suck him in a quieter rhythm while appreciating his low moans. I noted he especially enjoyed when I caressed beneath the head of his shaft with my tongue.

Don had also decelerated with his cropping of my butt cheeks. They burned beautifully and I hoped I could sit down tomorrow during classes. Oh boy, the things I was doing just so I could pursue my dream of becoming a criminal defense lawyer for underprivileged minors. I was crazy for doing this sugar baby thing. I knew I was, and yet in my heart, I knew it was worth it in the end. Especially if I could get pleasure out of it along the way and so far so good.

Was I being naughty taking the easy way in making money to achieve my dreams? Or was I being selfish in wanting pleasure and getting paid for it? Tonight was the closest I'd come to orgasming at a man's hands. I hoped I would be able to truly climax and not have to fake it with these two men.

I gasped as Don's warm hands suddenly melted over my hot ass cheeks.

"I'm going to pull out the plug, Liza. I just want you to give your full attention to Lloyd while I'm doing it."

I nodded jerkily. It wasn't easy for me to nod my head with a cock buried in my mouth. It wasn't easy to hold still either when I felt the butt plug suddenly move from deep within. I could literally feel every thick inch as Don gently pulled. I inhaled as the wide part of the plug left me and I whimpered at the sense of loss as he slowly kept pulling. I'd gotten used to having it buried inside of me and I didn't even realize it was out of me until my ass clenched empty air.

"Now, for some lube. It'll make it easier for me to penetrate you," Don whispered.

Lloyd's fingers tangled tighter in my hair and I realized I'd slacked off with my duty of pleasuring him, so I returned my attention to gently tightening my lips around his velvet-encased hard shaft. He groaned his appreciation and began to thrust in a most leisurely manner. It made me ponder exactly how many other women had he done this to, because he seemed to possess such self-control.

My thoughts turned to imagining Lloyd's shaft pistoning into my aching and needy vagina and I could feel my pussy tighten and the wetness of my excitement drenching my inner thighs. I could feel Don's lube-encased fingers dip into my anal channel and I focused on keeping my breathing steady as his fingers gently explored, prodding against my tight anal muscles as he smoothed the lube in and around. He massaged tenderly and I sighed when my constricted muscles relaxed a little more beneath his ministrations.

He slowly withdrew and I heard the slurp of lubrication as he squirted more out and then he slid some more lube into me with his fingers. His soft prodding had me moaning as a bunch of muscles deep inside of me loosened.

"Wow, she's really tight back here. She's going to be a challenge to take," Don murmured as he withdrew.

I felt my eyes widen. Had he just said it was going to be a challenge? A bit of a fright shot through me. What did he mean by that? Was his shaft going to be too big? Was it going to hurt?

I forced my fear aside. That's what the lube was for. To help prevent friction and to make it more comfortable for both parties during the penetrations. At least that's what Jaz had told me when we'd discussed anal. Since she'd done it before, I'd asked her a lot of questions and I'd also done some online research to be mentally ready.

Despite thinking I'd been prepared, being confronted with the real thing was, well, shall we say, challenging.

"She's really exciting me with her sweet mouth. I can't hold off much longer, Don," I heard Lloyd mutter in a taut voice.

He'd really slowed down in his thrusts now and I began to feel an overwhelming urge to grab his shaft and bring it into my pussy. I realized now why I had been restrained. It had to be because they'd wanted to prevent me from getting what I wanted. Being denied was increasing my urge for sex and maybe it was to stop me from forcing the pleasure onto myself too.

They wanted to be in control.

But their control over me was starting to make me seriously needy. A sweet anxiety was washing over me. My lips were bruised and felt so unbelievably big. My buttocks were seething hot. My breasts and nipples were ultra-sensitive and my ass and pussy craved to be taken.

"I hear you, baby. All this cropping and watching her breasts and ass blush has gotten me harder than I've ever been before." Don answered.

Lloyd chuckled. "And I know from experience how much you like to crop."

"When Liza goes home, I'll be cropping that nice cock of yours," Don said in a sultry voice.

Oh my goodness. It appeared Don had a cropping fetish.

"I look forward to it," Lloyd answered in a low sexy tone.

I gazed up at Lloyd and my heart clenched at the sweet way he was looking at Don. I blinked with wonder. How long had these two men been together? It was so obvious now to me. It was in the caring way they looked at each other that cemented the idea that these two men were a couple. Why hadn't I noticed it right from the beginning?

Okay, yep, definitely something going on between these two men.

I forced my thoughts back to myself as another round of lube was pressed into me. My ass was reacting to his stimulation now. Clenching and unclenching up a storm and in turn my pussy was starting in on the action too!

I wanted to yell at them. Wanted to shout and say *excuse me, but I'd like to get an orgasm here!*

"She's ready," Don suddenly said as he withdrew his fingers.

She's ready.

Those two words tumbled around in my mind like a whirlwind as Lloyd withdrew his shaft from my mouth and then undid my cuff restraints. He held out his hand to me. He was like some naked gentleman asking me to dance, and my arm felt so heavy as I gladly clasped his hot palm.

He was a strong man as he helped me off the sofa with ease. I felt so wobbly as I stood. Weak and submissive. I'd turned into an entirely different person than I'd been before tonight's escapade had started. Before tonight, I was an innocent and curious young woman, now I was insane with need and I wanted satisfaction. I was a tiger in heat.

My entire body trembled as Lloyd led me away from the black sofa toward the king-sized canopied bed where Don stood casually removing the rest of his clothing. He possessed plenty of muscles. I could tell that he looked after himself. Lloyd did too. Both men were physically fit for guys in their thirties.

The canopied bed looked gorgeous. It was draped with a decorative sheer white material that was pulled toward the four black metal corner posts and tied back with large sheer white bows. The comforters and pillows were shades of white and light grey. It looked like a bed made for a princess, but I felt nothing like royalty at the moment.

A princess could and would demand her men to service her and bring her to orgasm the instant she wanted it. But I couldn't demand. I had to remember why I was here. To pleasure Don and it appeared to pleasure Lloyd too. I had no doubt Lloyd would be my sugar daddy as well. It was in the sizzling way the two men looked at me. Like I was their possession.

Besides, I doubted Don would want Lloyd to be with another woman without Don being present. And vice versa. Of course those were just my instincts and I could be mistaken, but I didn't think so.

I tensed as Lloyd stepped in front of me. His gaze scorched my senses. His blue eyes were blazing with lust. His eyelids so heavy lidded, he almost looked like he might be asleep. But he was far from it as his warm palms settled upon my hips and he held me tight. In turn I settled my hands on his waist, relishing the heat from his body against my fingers.

I trembled as he pressed his upper half against me. His chiselled chest melted against my breasts, his muscles creating a scorching pressure on my ultra-tenderized nipples. His head lowered and his succulent mouth melted over mine giving my senses quite a bang.

My hips jerked in response but his sturdy hands held me tight, preventing me from fully bucking.

I moaned as he pushed his cockhead against my ultra-sensitive clitoris, creating an array of sensations; pleasure, anticipation and need. My mind splintered as he began massaging my clit with his grape-shaped cockhead.

Chapter Six

I t felt so wonderful to have his smooth, hot flesh rubbing and circling my eager little bundle of nerves and then he'd dip down to tease against my wet vaginal opening, collecting my juices and bringing his big cockhead back to massage some more. The impact of his flesh upon my flesh had me gasping within the crashing waves of need that he was so perfectly building.

Yes, I could tell Lloyd was experienced. He knew how to get a woman's body humming. He knew the art of foreplay. It's exactly what I did when I masturbated. I slowly built the pleasure until it consumed me. Just like Lloyd was doing with his passionate kisses and teasing touches on my quivering clit.

Don's hands slid along my sides and he held me firm. I gasped as his mushroom-shaped cockhead pushed against my aching sphincter. I sensed he wore a condom and somewhere deep in my brain I thought that was a good idea. It would keep him protected. But that thought disintegrated as my ass was on fire and my anal canal was still clenching from all his naughty cropping.

Man, I couldn't wait for him to take me back there. I wanted to feel his strong hot length burrowing deep inside of me.

"She's going to be tight, just like I expected," Don muttered as he brushed his warm lips in an array of feather-like kisses along my upper back. The tender touches sparked shards of pleasure upon my flesh.

"The tighter the better," Lloyd mumbled from around my eager lips.

I was kissing him back now. Desperation making me frenzied. I was wild and full of anticipation at the idea of two cocks threatening to enter me at any moment.

I'd never felt so alive before. So full of hunger and passion.

The intimate way both cocks were caressing my entrances was destroying any control I might still be holding onto. The two men were making my entire body heat up like an inferno.

No longer was it just my breasts and ass being hot, but *all* of me was burning and yearning to come.

I was moaning as we kept kissing. Every nerve ending in my entire being was ablaze and I was on fire.

Then Lloyd suddenly pulled away and I whimpered my distress.

To my surprise I heard the sounds of kissing near my right ear. My eyes flew open and I did a double take at what was happening.

Lloyd and Don were kissing. Their mouths were melding together right over my shoulder!

I was sandwiched right in the middle of the two of them, my need for release just about my undoing and here they were kissing like I didn't even exist.

But the two cocks thickening against my intimate parts surely indicated they were into each other. Big time.

Lloyd and Don kissed for what seemed like forever. Their aroused moans and harsh groans split through the air like erotic music.

I just couldn't believe it.

Personally I'd never seen two men kissing before and I found it quite intriguing, yet frustrating on my part for being ignored in this way.

Finally they drew apart. And acting as if nothing had just happened, both men continued teasing my entrances.

A cockhead nudged against my back door and a cockhead pressed at my vaginal opening.

I was panting now, my excitement back two-fold. I wondered when they were going to take me.

"Did you enjoy that interlude?" Don whispered into my left ear.

I swear I wanted to tell him off, but I needed to remain professional. "Yes," I hissed.

My frustration must have come through in my voice though because Don and Lloyd both chuckled.

Bastards.

"Take her," Don suddenly whispered beneath his breath.

Before I could even blink or decipher the order Don had just given to Lloyd, Lloyd thrust his cock into me like it was a speeding missile. Thankfully I was soaked and slippery, allowing for a fast entrance without any pain.

I gasped at the unexpectedly quick and utterly thick intrusion. I thought for sure I would climax upon the first penetration, but the friction just wasn't enough for me to come. I suspected he knew exactly what he was doing and he wouldn't make me come until he wanted me to come.

I dug my fingers deeper into his muscles, holding him tighter.

Lloyd withdrew and then Don pushed his ultra-big shaft into my quivering ass. Not too far in, just a couple of inches, but enough for me to thank goodness he'd lubed me so nicely that he was penetrating me without issue.

But, oh boy, the fullness of him was exquisite and I was gasping from the invasion! His partial shaft was so hot and it throbbed like a possessive brand inside of me. To my surprise, it felt so wonderfully good.

Oh yes, stay inside. I really enjoy this fullness. Please, stay in, an inner voice begged inside my head.

But he withdrew.

Oh no!

Then Lloyd was entering me, pushing deeper into my clenching vagina. My pussy welcomed him. My wet muscles wrapped around him like a glove.

So tight around him. So nice. Just like he belonged inside of me.

My senses spun as he withdrew.

Don entered. Further this time.

I trembled at the pressure of his penis. It was like a steel pole pressing into my virgin ass and suddenly I panicked and writhed and tried to get away as he burrowed deeper than before. He was so big and I was suddenly so afraid as my muscles protested and there was the slightest tinge of pain.

"Just relax," Don whispered easily. "I know what I'm doing. You'll be fine. You'll love it. Just give it a minute. Your ass will submit. Trust me."

Easy for Don to tell me to relax. He didn't have a cock buried up his ass at the moment!

I nodded jerkily.

But he was right. The pain did subside and the shudders of need flooded back. The pleasure was mounting.

I could feel it. I was getting tenser. I wanted release.

Impulsively I began to keen.

Don gave me a string of butterfly kisses with his scorching lips across my upper back. It felt beautiful. I guess it was an effort to distract me.

I gripped Lloyd's waist even tighter as the tension in me mounted.

My fingers dug into his taut muscles and I was surprised he didn't cry out in pain as I was holding onto him so hard. He picked that moment to fuse his mouth over my lips, sending fissures of pleasure throughout my entire body.

Lloyd's mouth ravished mine and I felt heady.

I hadn't even realized that Don was penetrating my behind even deeper and that their succulent kisses upon my flesh was a distraction technique! If I hadn't been so overwhelmed I'd be joking with them that I was onto their game.

But I couldn't talk, even if my life depended on it. Heck, I don't think I would have even been able to form words as I was too busy focusing on the intense pressure spearing into my ass.

This full feeling was different. It was something I'd never experienced before and to my surprise there were incredible sensations of pleasure rippling deep inside as my ass began to clench around the thick intrusion of heated flesh.

I moaned my appreciation. I could feel the spiral of losing my self-control. It was spreading like a wildfire.

Don withdrew slowly and softly and then Lloyd thrust into my pussy, fast and profound.

The two men were total opposites in the way they penetrated me.

Don, careful and gentle, whereas Lloyd was rough and deep. I discovered I liked both approaches.

They began a steady rhythm, pounding one cock into me at a time. Kind of like a see-saw motion.

Oh have mercy! This was exciting and way so intense. The erotic pleasure spread.

Perspiration was beading up everywhere on my skin. I was breathing rough and harsh. Breathing so fast it hurt.

My entire body felt so rigid and I was perched at the edge of the pleasure cliff. I sensed something was going to give. It had to. If it didn't, I would surely go insane.

Instinctively I began bucking. The thuds of flesh slapping against flesh shot through the air like bullets. The slurps of wet sex ripped through the room as one cock withdrew from one tight orifice and the other shaft plunged into another opening. The sounds intermingled with their guttural groans and my sexy moans.

Gosh, I'd never made noises like that before. I sounded like a woman who was truly enjoying herself.

My thoughts were suddenly not processing as their thrusts quickened.

Oh yes, I could feel myself about to enter the pleasure zone. I was just about there and then there was just the perfect friction that I needed and I was over and into where I needed to be.

The climax slammed into me like jolts of electricity and a whirlwind of pleasure sucked me right into a wicked vortex where I lost any and all self-control. I became a gyrating maniac between the two men.

I screamed as I shattered. Cried out as I exploded into a frenzy.

Their driving cocks rocked sizzling spasms into me. Their hot kisses sent tremors deep into my being. I lost all sense of me as I was quickly swallowed into bliss.

Oh yes, waves and waves of blessed bliss. It raged all around me. Inside of me. On me.

I never wanted to come out, so I held onto the reigns.

They kept pumping into me. Two hard, delicious cocks driving into me, now at the same time. They kept thrusting until I flew from one climax right into another one.

Sweet mercy! It was so good.

Then they were licking my shoulders. Biting gently into the sides of my neck. Nibbling on my earlobes.

Their intimate mouths and cocks drove me into a third climax.

Now I understood what it truly meant to orgasm. My masturbating had been nothing compared to this body wrenching, soul-loving pleasure. I must have died and gone to heaven as I shuddered and spasmed and stayed wrapped inside the bliss for as long as I could.

Vaguely I could feel their hard, sweaty bodies tense. Their cocks jerk. Then hot jets of sperm began to pump into my ass as Don's penis exploded inside of me. A moment later Lloyd came into me like an out-of-control inferno.

By the time the searing convulsions that had tangled throughout my body subsided and ebbed, I was dazed and weak.

Yet, I felt like a million bucks.

Whatever I'd just experienced over and over, I wanted it again and again.

I was hooked onto these two men; I knew I would do this many more times even if I never got paid!

Thankfully, they held tight to me as they withdrew their spent cocks. If they hadn't been holding me up, surely I would have dropped to the floor like a rag doll.

I heard them whisper to each other. Something about getting me into bed.

One of the men picked me up and laid me upon the soft, delightful sheets. Then the mattress moved on each side of me as they climbed into bed with me. Warm comforters were splashed over me and they cradled me.

I was incredibly excited from having orgasmed so completely and for so many times, that my heart was racing and I was panting between my parted lips.

As we lay beneath the comforters, I felt their hands clasp together over my belly. The two men held hands and I felt their hot gazes on me.

I opened my eyes to find them looking at me. Perspiration dampened their hair. Their faces were flushed red and they had big happy grins plastered on their faces.

"You were perfect, Liza. Better than I ever imagined," Don said softly.

I closed my eyes and smiled. I was so glad that they'd had a great time with me. But I was so incredibly tired and I had to go to school in the morning. I would have to get up early and head back to my place to shower and change.

Somewhere in the back of my mind I knew I should tell them to set the alarm so I wouldn't be late. But I just couldn't bring myself to speak.

I truly was incredibly spent.

"So? What do you think, Lloyd," I heard Don whisper. "Do you want her as your sugar baby too?"

I knew it! I knew Don wouldn't want Lloyd with another woman. He wanted Lloyd with us.

I felt pleased and held my breath as I awaited his answer.

"Baby boy, she was my sugar baby the instant I saw her with you," Lloyd replied.

I felt the men squeeze each others' hands. It was an incredibly endearing gesture and it brought happiness to my heart.

It was okay that they didn't ask if it was acceptable to me to have two sugar daddies.

Heck, even if they did ask, there was no way I was going to say no because I had loved being taken by two sugar daddies.

The End

Jasmine Black
~Erotica~Without the
Romance

Here are some more Jasmine Black stories...

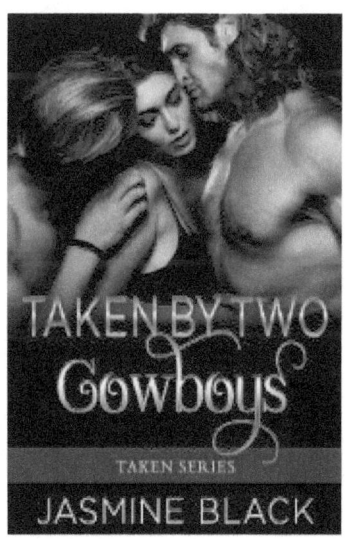

Taken by Two Cowboys

———— ⌾ ————

Sierra Allan works hard at her late-father's horse ranch. When her step-brother adds her handy girl services to a private auction to help raise money for the failing ranch, she figures there's no harm...but she's stunned when her services are sold to two sexy cowboys who give her an erotic way to save the ranch—submitting to their dark desires..

Taken by Three Billionaires

Billionaire friends, Liam, Theo and Elijah have just won Princess
Isabella in a billionaire card game. Isabella knows exactly what the three
men will want from her...she just hadn't expected to have all three of
them at once!

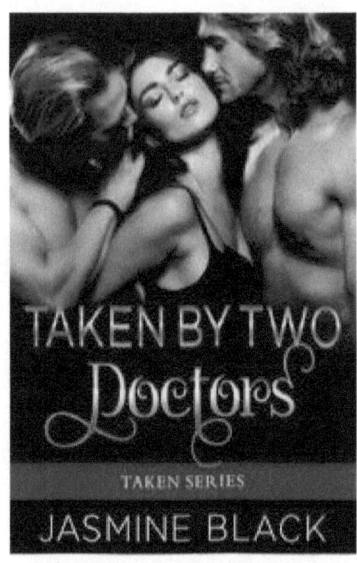

Taken by Two Doctors
A BDSM Medical Fetish Erotica Quickie MFM

Waitress Jean Spelling visits her controversial doctor once a month for some much-needed...stress relief. She looks forward to putting her feet up in the stirrups and enjoys Dr. Ball's naughty unconventional treatments. This time when she arrives, she's surprised to discover that she'll be physically examined by two doctors and they'll prescribe her some much-needed release right there on the examination table!

Stories in Jasmine Black's Ménage series

Stories in Jasmine Black's Taken series

Taken by Two Prison Guards
Taken by Two Elves
Taken by Two Mountain Men
Taken by Two Cops
Taken by Two Santas
Taken by Two Lifeguards
Taken by Two Firefighters
Taken by Two Bikers
Taken by Two Billionaires
Taken by Two Bosses
Taken by Two Cowboys
Taken by Two Personal Trainers
Taken by Two Carpenters
Taken by Two Sugar Daddies

Jasmine Black Website ~ http://www.jasmine-black.com
Twitter ~ @blackerotica1

Jasmine Black also writes as Jan Springer!

If you like romance with your erotica, try Jan Springer.

———————— ⟨∞⟩ ————————

Jan Springer ~ Erotic Romance

Cowboys For Christmas
Cowboys Online 1 ~ Moose Ranch
Jan Springer

A Canadian Contemporary Ménage Romance m/f/m/m Series

Jennifer Jane (JJ) Watson has spent the past ten Christmases in a maximum-security prison.

The last thing she expects is to get early parole, along with a job on a remote Canadian cattle ranch serving Christmas holiday dinners to three of the sexiest cowboys she's ever met!

Rafe, Brady and Dan thought they were getting a couple of male ex-cons to help out around their secluded ranch, but instead they get an attractive and very appealing female.

In the snowbound wilds of Northern Ontario, female companionship is rare.

It's a good thing the three men like to share...

They're dominating, sexy-as-sin and they fill JJ with the hottest ménage fantasies she's ever had. Suddenly she's craving cowboys for Christmas and wishing for something she knows she can never have...a happily ever after.

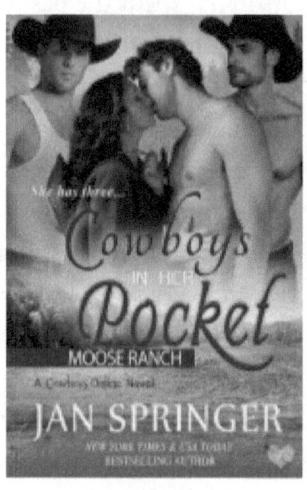

Cowboys In Her Pocket
Cowboys Online 2 ~ Moose Ranch
Jan Springer

*After spending ten years in a maximum-security prison Jennifer Jane (JJ)
Watson got early parole and a job on a remote Canadian cattle ranch
playing housekeeper to three of the sexiest cowboys she's ever met...*

Spring has finally arrived at Moose Ranch, and a single woman fresh out
of prison shouldn't be experiencing scorching ménages with her three
sexy-as-sin cowboys. But JJ's love for her men continues to grow as she
gives into the fevered heat and scorching passions she feels for each of
them.

Life is perfect.

Until her new life is tested when mysterious happenings occur on the
ranch and then one of her cowboys is viciously attacked and injured.

Will JJ's newfound freedom and happiness be ripped away?

*Rafe, Brady and Dan never expected to find an attractive and very
appealing female to help them out at their secluded ranch. But in the wilds
of Northern Ontario, female companionship is rare. It's a good thing the
three men like to share...*

Brady, Dan and Rafe have never been happier. Their cattle ranch is flourishing and their continued desire to share the sexy woman who cares for them makes their life complete. Until danger threatens to rip everything apart...

Loving Her Cowboys
Cowboys Online 3 ~ Moose Ranch
Jan Springer

AFTER SPENDING TEN years in a maximum-security prison Jennifer Jane (JJ) Watson got early parole and a job on a remote Canadian cattle ranch playing housekeeper to three of the sexiest cowboys she's ever met...

Her love for her cowboys continues to grow as she gives into fevered heat. But JJ's simmering restlessness explodes and she's seriously making up for lost time by pursuing her dreams. There's only one little problem. She hasn't revealed to her bosses what she's been up to while they're away tending to the cattle. She knows when they discover her secret, there will be hell to pay.

Ranchers Rafe, Dan and Brady have found the woman who completes them. She makes their secluded ranch a home-sweet-home. She's vulnerable, sweet and willing to share her bed with all three of them. But when JJ's secret is unwittingly revealed, they're stunned and angry. They figure it's time to dole out some fiery punishment in some mighty naughty ways...

Cowboys In Her Heart
Cowboys Online #4

AFTER SPENDING TEN years in a maximum-security prison, JJ gets unexpected parole and a job on a Canadian ranch serving up scrumptious dinners and lots of hot love to three of the sexiest cowboys she's ever met.

Jennifer Jane "JJ" Watson has never been happier. She's going to have a baby!

Thankfully, their wilderness ranch is a nice distraction for her three sexy cowboys while she's away flying her plane. But when she's home, her dominant hunks are tending to her naughty pregnant cravings and that includes plenty of sizzling ménages.

Rafe, Brady and Dan don't much like the idea of their woman flying the Canadian skies and being at the mercy of the unpredictable Northern Ontario weather. They would prefer having her warming their beds twenty-four seven. But she has a way of getting what she wants and right now she needs her new-found freedom.

Worst fears are realized when JJ, her friend and JJ's plane suddenly go missing and she doesn't come back home to them.

Always Her Cowboys
Cowboys Online 5 ~ Moose Ranch

1

Reader Advisory: Best to read in order. 1. Cowboys for Christmas, 2. Cowboys in Her Pocket, 3. Loving Her Cowboys, 4.Cowboys in Her Heart, 5. Always Her Cowboys. 6. Her Forever Cowboys 7. Claiming Her Cowboys

A Canadian Contemporary Ménage Romance m/f/m/m

JENNIFER JANE (JJ) Watson has spent ten Christmases in a maximum-security prison. The last thing she expected was to get early parole, along with a job on a remote Canadian cattle ranch serving Christmas holiday dinners to three of the sexiest cowboys she's ever met!

Rafe, Brady and Dan thought they were getting male ex-cons to help out around their secluded ranch, but instead they got an attractive and very appealing female. In the snowbound wilds of Northern Ontario, female companionship is rare. It's a good thing the three men like to share...

Christmas is coming once again to Moose Ranch and with JJ's due date approaching, she's distracting herself from anxiety attacks by keeping herself ultra-busy preparing for the arrival of her baby and planning Moose Ranch's first annual Christmas party!

1. https://janspringerauthor.files.wordpress.com/2017/11/alwayshercowboys_ebook-1new.jpg

In having a wee baby on the way, there's a lot of stress for Brady, Rafe and Dan. Especially due to JJ's decision on having a wilderness mid-wife deliver the baby *at their secluded ranch* - with *all* of them present for the birth! But their concerns don't stop the men from showing JJ how much they love her...out of bed and in!

With wicked snowstorms, a grounded bush plane, a cheerful holiday party and a sweet baby on the way, the owners of Moose Ranch know this will be one sparkling Christmas season they won't soon forget...

PLUS: HER FOREVER COWBOYS ~ Snowy Creek Ranch #1 Cowboys Online #6 &

Claiming Her Cowboys ~ Moose Ranch #6 Cowboys Online #7

Risqué Girl Delights Boxed Set
(Contemporary Erotic Romance)

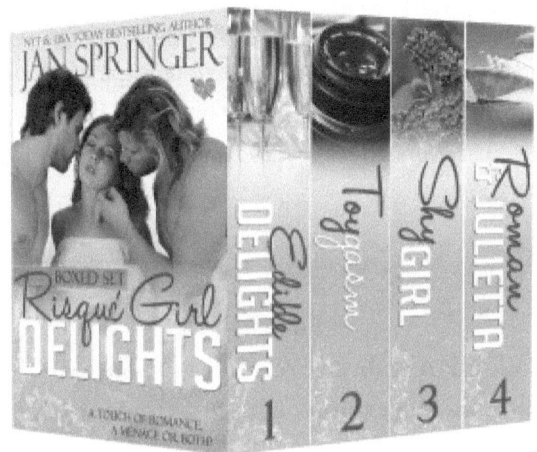

2

...a touch of romance, a ménage or both?

Edible Delights

YEARS AGO ALLIE MASTERS lost herself in the scorching passion of a ménage a trois relationship with her two bosses. In order to regain her independence, she walked away.

Max and Nick were very fulfilled with their gorgeous assistant. The lovemaking was breathtaking and both men willingly shared the woman they wanted to spend the rest of their lives with. Then she left.

Now Max and Nick have decided it's time to seduce Allie back into their lives.

Toygasm

IT'S A CASE OF MISTAKEN identity when the two owners of Sexy Toys, show up for an erotic several day photo shoot of their toys with famous nude model Cammie Creek.

2. https://janspringerauthor.files.wordpress.com/2015/02/rgdelights_box_js_3d_noshadow-1.jpg

Cammie believes the two hunks are the male models she's supposed to work with. Usually she doesn't mix business with pleasure, but when they're seducing her right there in front of the camera, she can't resist turning them into her own personal naughty toys.

Josh and Jode are enjoying the perks of being male models; hot lust, sizzling toys and the best pleasure they've ever had. But how will Cammie react when she discovers they're actually her bosses and not just male models?

Shy Girl

FINALLY FREE OF AN abusive relationship, "Shy Girl" Emma McCall sheds her inhibitions and explores her sensual side at Club Rendezvous, a club specializing in the Alternate Lifestyle.

At the club she's surprised to find Logan Masters, a sexy hunk she's secretly fantasized about since college. With Logan's help, Emma will experience her ultimate fantasy - a scorching ménage a trois.

Roman and Julietta

HER PERFECT LOVER...

Modern day pirate Julietta Black's life has always been immersed in the violent and traditional ways of piracy. When her family's arch enemy puts a hit out on her family, Julietta knows there's only one way to lift the hit; she must kidnap the enemy's sexy grandson and force a union between the two warring families. Night after night, wrapped in Roman's strong arms, she can't deny the searing attraction blazing between them. Nor can she deny he now holds her heart as well as her life in his hands.

His dream angel...

When Roman Prince's mysterious captor offers him a luscious woman to bed, fierce desire ignites, melting his usually tight self-control. Lust quickly turns to love as he enjoys their naughty trysts more than he should. How will he react when he discovers he's been kidnapped, not for a ransom, but captured for his sperm?

Alpha Outlaws Boxed Set (Books 1-5 Outlaw Lovers)
5 Books!!
Reader Advisory: Sensitive Readers beware of triggers in "Tyler's Woman"

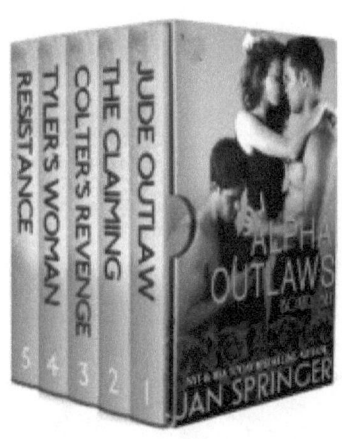

3

IN A WORLD GONE MAD...

A fast-acting virus has killed a majority of the world's female population. With the creation of The Claiming Law, groups of men suddenly have the right to claim a female as their sensual property and the sexy Outlaw brothers are going to declare ownership of the women they love...any way they can.

Jude Outlaw

When Cate Callahan learns Jude is coming home from the Terrorist Wars and is ready to claim her under the new law—with the help of his four brothers—she steals their boat and escapes to the high seas. Unfortunately, her runaway bid for freedom doesn't last long.

Quickly capturing his lover, Jude rekindles the flames and seduces Cate back into his bed.

But Jude holds a secret that could make him lose Cate forever...
PLUS

The Claiming

Seeking refuge from the Claiming Law, Callie Callahan hides in a deserted cabin in the Maine woods and is shocked when her ex-flame finds her. She's always craved being in Luke Outlaw's arms. Tasting him. Touching him. Taking him deeply within her. So, what's a girl to do but to delve into the sinful delights he offers.

Luke has finally reunited with the love of his life. He knows there is only one way to keep Callie safe and with him forever. He'll do it with the help of his three brothers and an assortment of naughty toys. Rekindling the flames between them, he unleashes Callie's sensual side, taking her in ways she never dreamed possible, all with the ultimate goal of introducing her to the Outlaw Lovers and The Claiming.

Colter's Revenge

Revenge belongs to Dr. Colter Outlaw when he unexpectedly reunites with the beautiful woman who broke his heart during the Terrorist Wars. Capturing her, collaring her and holding her against her will, he seduces her, fills her with wicked desires and naughty cravings for a delicious ménage. Fully intent on breaking her heart and walking away, Colter's plans unravel when he submits to the carnal pleasures Ashley gives him so freely.

Colter had told her he loved her. He'd whispered promises of rescue from her life as a slave, but when he'd suddenly disappeared, she'd been devastated. Infected with a version of the X-virus that leaves Ashley Blakely sexually excited on a daily basis, she has come to Pleasure Palace to bid on a cure for her illness. She never expected her Outlaw Lover to be there and screw her plans. Nor did she expect to give him her heart and body so easily...

Tyler's Woman

For years Tyler Outlaw and his best friend, Hunter Brown, endured brutal torture and worse in an overseas terrorist prison. Finally, free of their hell, they return home intent on seducing Laurie into their erotic-filled fantasies.

Laurie Callahan has always experienced red-hot pleasure and passionate love in Tyler Outlaw's arms. But when he's pronounced MIA, presumed dead in the Terrorist Wars, Laurie's world is shattered, and her heart is broken.

Shocked to discover Tyler is alive and he's taken a male lover, Laurie is thrust into a sensual world of sizzling seductions, scorching ménages and the carnal desires that both scarred men crave. But she fears Tyler won't want her when he discovers she's not the same woman he left behind...

****READER CAUTION IS ADVISED (m/m forced scenes) ****

Resistance

In the near future, a virus has been unleashed, killing a majority of the world's female population, forcing the introduction of the Claiming Law. A law that states men have all the rights and women are sexual property claimable by groups of men.

Fugitive female...

Renegade Resistance leader Reena "Red" Wilde is in for the fight of her life when she experiences an erotic attraction to the two most dangerous men she's ever met.

Black ops assassin...

Months ago, Will "Blade" Smith spent one sizzling evening in the arms of a red-haired seductress. Now she's his next assignment. One look into her gorgeous eyes and he's wrestling his heated cravings for her all over again.

Bounty Hunter...

When Cade Outlaw nabs his bounty, sexy-as-sin Reena Wilde, his profession dictates she's hands-off. But he can't ignore the magnetic sparks between them...or that she is the biggest temptation of his life.

Resistance is futile...

After Reena escapes Cade and Will and falls prey to a band of evil hunters, she's grateful her sexy hunks come to her rescue...and in return, saves their lives. Trapped in a solitary cabin during a wicked snowstorm, she can't resist her two, well-hung studs, nor can she deny they've claimed her heart.

Many more Jasmine Black and Jan Springer electronic books, print books, audiobooks plus translated electronic books and print books can be found at http://www.janspringer.com and http://www.jasmine-black.com

Here are ways we can connect:

Jasmine Black Website at http://janspringerauthor.wordpress.com/jasmine-black/

Jan Springer Website at http://www.janspringer.com[1]

Instagram – http://www.instagram.com/janspringerauthor

Facebook - https://www.facebook.com/janspringereroticromance

Twitter Jan Springer- https://twitter.com/janspringer @janspringer

Twitter Jasmine Black - https://twitter.com/blackerotica1 @blackerotica1

Pinterest - http://www.pinterest.com/janspringer2/

Jan's Blog - http://janspringerauthor.wordpress.com/blog-2/

Happy Reading,

Jasmine Black / Jan Springer

---

1.   http://www.janspringer.com/

Other stories in the Taken Series by Jasmine Black:

Taken by Two Doctors, Taken by Three Doctors, Taken by Two Bikers, Taken by Three Bikers, Taken by Two Billionaires, Taken by Three Billionaires, Taken by Two Bosses, Taken by Two Cowboys, Taken by Three Cowboys, Taken by Two Firefighters, Taken by Two Carpenters, Taken by Two Personal Trainers, Taken by Two Santas, Taken by Three Bodyguards, Taken by Two Cops, Taken by Two Prison Guards, Taken by Two Lifeguards, Taken by Two Mountain Men, Taken by Two Elves and more!

Don't miss out!

Visit the website below and you can sign up to receive emails whenever Jasmine Black publishes a new book. There's no charge and no obligation.

https://books2read.com/r/B-A-GIJD-ZVNKC

BOOKS 2 READ

Connecting independent readers to independent writers.